# Pearl Learns A Lesson

MERVIN THE WIZARD
DO NOT DISTURB

Written by
Laura Appleton-Smith

Illustrated by
Carol Vredenburgh

**Laura Appleton-Smith** holds a degree in English from Middlebury College.
Laura is a primary school teacher who has combined her talents in creative writing with
her experience in early childhood education to create *Books to Remember*.
She lives in New Hampshire with her husband, Terry.

**Carol Vredenburgh** graduated Summa Cum Laude from Syracuse University and has worked
as an artist and illustrator ever since. This is the third book she has illustrated for Flyleaf Publishing.

## A Book to Remember™
Published by Flyleaf Publishing
Post Office Box 287, Lyme, NH 03768

For orders or information, contact us at **(800) 449-7006**.
Please visit our website at **www.flyleafpublishing.com**

Third Edition 12/09
Library of Congress Catalog Card Number: 2002090758
Hard cover ISBN-13: 978-1-929262-13-7
Soft cover ISBN-13: 978-1-929262-14-4
Printed and bound in the USA at Worzalla Publishing, Stevens Point, WI. 12/09

*For Carol, thank you for sharing your talents with us over the years.*
*Great things can come from holiday party conversations;*
*and personal discoveries do happen through the creation of books!*

*LAS*

*To the Pearl in all of us.*

*CV*

# Chapter One

Once upon a time, a king and queen had an infant girl named Pearl.

To the king and queen, Pearl was a gift grander than any.
One day she would inherit their kingdom.

As Pearl got bigger she was given every gift she asked for.

Her bed was bigger than any bed in the kingdom.
Her closet was filled with dresses and skirts.

Pearl was a lucky girl.

Pearl began each day by jumping on her bed.
She twirled and jumped until her mattress burst
and bits of fluff puffed up and swirled around her.

She pulled on her dolls until their legs ripped off,
then she hurled them from her bed.

When Pearl rang a silver bell
a servant ran in with her snack.

Pearl dripped jam and butter on her quilts.
She spilled urns of milk on her rug.

When she was full she burped;
then she went to her closet to get dressed.

## Chapter Two

One day Pearl dressed herself in a red velvet dress. She put on silk stockings and black velvet slippers. At last, she hung a silver locket from her neck.

Pearl was perfect.

As she left she told the servants to fix the things
she had ripped and cracked and bent.
Then she went to visit the king and queen.

Pearl flirted with the king and queen.
She kissed and hugged them and then she asked for her next gift,
"I want a dog with soft black fur and a silver collar."

The king and queen were alert to the fact
that Pearl did not respect her gifts.

At last, the king told Pearl,
"No. Not until you learn to respect the gifts you have."

This was the first time Pearl had ever been told no.

She burst up from the king's lap.
She blurted out bad words.
She hurled herself onto the rug and kicked and ranted,
but the king and queen were firm. "No."

# Chapter Three

Pearl was so mad she ran from the kingdom.
She ran until her legs hurt and her lungs burned.
When she stopped to rest she spotted the words
"Mervin the Wizard DO NOT DISTURB," printed on a fir tree.

Pearl smirked, "A wizard..."
She rapped her hand on the trunk of the fir tree.
Pearl heard a man yell, "NO VISITORS!"
Pearl, being Pearl, went in regardless.

Mervin the Wizard was not a bit bigger than Pearl.
He was dressed in rags and bits of fur.
He smelled of fungus and dirt.

Pearl gasped, but remembering he was a wizard she asked,
"Will you help a damsel in distress?"

Mervin grunted.

Pearl went on, "This is a list of things I want."
She pulled a long list from the pocket in her skirt.

"You can cast a spell and grant me my list. The first gift I want
is a dog with soft black fur and a silver collar."

Mervin spotted the locket on Pearl's neck.
"For the locket I will cast the spell,
but you must do the tasks I ask to be granted your gift."

Mervin was clever. Pearl handed him the locket.

# Chapter Four

Mervin went to his pit of burning logs.

Into his bubbling pot he added:
a rotten turnip, a clump of dirt,
a fluff of dandruff, and a handful of worms.

As he stirred the pot he murmured the words,
"Abracadabra, nimbus nitwit nist,
grant this girl the first gift on her list."

Mervin dunked a goblet into the pot and handed it to Pearl, "Drink it."

Pearl gasped. The liquid smelled of mud.
It had worms swimming in it and flecks of dandruff on the top.

Pearl felt sick, but remembering her list she slurped the drink.
Mervin winked.

"Next you must work. Fill this sack with logs.
My dog Pepper will help you," Mervin told her.

Pepper got up from under the bed.
His fur was twisted with twigs and matted with dirt.
He smelled as bad as Mervin.

# Chapter Five

"You are the worst dog I have ever met,"
Pearl told Pepper as they went to hunt for logs.

"My dog will have fur as soft as velvet
and will smell better than a bed of herbs.
My dog will have a silver collar on its neck."

Pepper jumped up to lick Pearl's hand,
but as he did Pearl yelled, "Get back!"

Pepper slunk back from the girl.

Pearl grumbled as she picked up logs
to fill the sack. As each log was
dropped in the sack got bigger.

This perplexed Pearl and
she got madder and madder
as the sack got bigger and bigger.

When the sack was full it was bigger than Pearl.
It stuck on rocks and twigs as she dragged it.
Pearl yelled bad words. Birds lifted from the trees.
Animals scattered into the bracken and ferns.

"Stack the logs next to the pit," Mervin told Pearl when she got back.

As she stacked, Mervin dropped a pot and cracked it.
He stomped on a rung of his ladder and snapped it.
As he spilled a mug of grog on his rug he told her,
"When you have stacked the logs fix my pot and my ladder
and scrub the grog from my rug."

Pearl was flabbergasted.
"A spell is a spell," Mervin told her.

Pearl curled up next to the stack of logs and whimpered.
Pepper, being Pepper, went to comfort her
even after she had yelled at him.

At first Pearl turned her back on him,
but at last she lifted her hand and patted his matted fur.

Pearl felt better.
She got up and fixed the pot.
Pepper sat next to her.

Next she went to the ladder.
Pepper held the rung
as Pearl mended it.

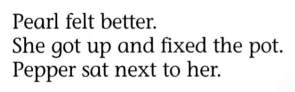

As Pearl scrubbed the rug, Pepper dropped a stick in front of her.
Pearl picked it up and tossed it. Pepper jumped to get it.

Mervin heard Pearl giggle as she tossed the stick a second time.
"Was Pearl's work fun?" Mervin wondered.

When Pearl had scrubbed the last drops of grog from the rug
Mervin dismissed her. He told Pearl to be back early the next day.
He would have her gift for her then.

Pearl asked if she could do one last task.

She filled a barrel with water and added a packet of herbs.

She dunked Pepper into the barrel.
She scrubbed the dirt from his fur
and picked the twigs from the mats he had.
Pepper was as soft as velvet.
He smelled of mint and lavender.

He was perfect.

# Chapter Six

Back in her big bed Pearl tossed and turned.
She thought about her gift of a dog with a silver collar.

In earnest, Pearl yearned that her dog
would be just like Pepper.

When Pearl got up the next day her back hurt from her work.
She did not jump on her bed.

She rang for her servants to bring in muffins and jam and milk.
Pearl did not spill her urn.
(She remembered the work of scrubbing Mervin's rug.)

The servants were flabbergasted.
Perhaps Pearl was ill?
She had turned into a different girl.

Pearl ran to Mervin's fir tree.
When she got there, Pepper sat next to Mervin,
as perfect as when she had left him.

Pepper wagged and wiggled when Pearl entered.
On his neck was her silver locket.

"You learned your lesson well, Pearl," Mervin told her.

"Your gift is Pepper–a dog with soft black fur and a silver collar. The king and queen understand you have earned this gift. Pepper may live with you in the kingdom forever."

Pearl promised Mervin that she and Pepper would visit him every day, and they did.

And they lived happily ever after.

*Pearl Learns a Lesson* is decodable with the knowledge of the 26 phonetic alphabet sounds, plus the "er" sound spelled with the "er," "ear," "ir," "ur," "or," and "ar" phonograms, and the ability to blend those sounds together.

**Puzzle Words** are words used in the story that are either irregular or have sound/spelling correspondences that the reader may not be familiar with.

The **Puzzle Word Review List** contains Puzzle Words that have been introduced in previous books in the *Books to Remember* Series.

*Please Note: If all of the words on this page are pre-taught and the reader knows the 26 phonetic alphabet sounds, plus the phonograms listed above, and has the ability to blend those sounds together, this book is 100% phonetically decodable.*

## Puzzle Word Review List:

| | |
|---|---|
| a | of |
| about | once |
| any | one |
| are | onto |
| around | out |
| as | pulled |
| be | put |
| been | queen |
| began | she |
| being | so |
| by | than |
| could | that |
| day | the |
| do | their |
| each | them |
| even | then |
| every | there |
| for | they |
| have | things |
| he | this |
| his | time |
| I | to |
| into | tree |
| is | visit |
| like | want |
| live | was |
| lived | were |
| may | when |
| me | with |
| my | would |
| named | you |
| no | your |

## Puzzle Words

forever
giggle
handful
happily
lucky
regardless
thought
told
water
whimpered

## "ar" Words

coll**ar**
wiz**ar**d

## "ear" Words

**ear**ly
**ear**ned
**ear**nest
h**ear**d
l**ear**n
l**ear**ned
P**ear**l
P**ear**l's
y**ear**ned

## "or" Words

comf**or**t
visit**or**s
w**or**ds
w**or**k
w**or**ms
w**or**st

## "er" Words

aft**er**
al**er**t
bett**er**
bigg**er**
butt**er**
clev**er**
diff**er**ent
ent**er**ed
ev**er**
f**er**ns
flabb**er**gasted
forev**er**
grand**er**
h**er**
h**er**bs
h**er**self
ladd**er**
lavend**er**
madd**er**
M**er**vin
M**er**vin's
Pepp**er**
p**er**fect
p**er**haps
p**er**plexed
rememb**er**ed
rememb**er**ing
scatt**er**ed
s**er**vant
silv**er**
slipp**er**s
und**er**
und**er**stand
wat**er**
whimp**er**ed
wond**er**ed

## "ur" Words

bl**ur**ted
b**ur**ned
b**ur**ning
b**ur**ped
b**ur**st
c**ur**led
dist**ur**b
f**ur**
h**ur**led
h**ur**t
m**ur**mured
sl**ur**ped
t**ur**ned
t**ur**nip
**ur**ns

## "ir" Words

b**ir**ds
d**ir**t
f**ir**
f**ir**m
f**ir**st
fl**ir**ted
g**ir**l
sk**ir**ts
sm**ir**ked
st**ir**red
sw**ir**led
tw**ir**led